CareBears
FALL FUN

By Justin Spelvin
Illustrated by Jeff Albrecht Studios

ISBN 0-439-78539-1
CARE BEARS™ characters and designs © 2005 Those Characters From Cleveland, Inc.
Used under license by Scholastic Inc. All rights reserved.
Published by Scholastic Inc. SCHOLASTIC and associated logos are trademarks and/or registered trademarks of Scholastic Inc.
12 11 10 9 8 7 6 5 4 3 2 1   5 6 7 8 9/0
Printed in the U.S.A.
First printing, October 2005

SCHOLASTIC INC.

New York   Toronto   London   Auckland   Sydney
Mexico City   New Delhi   Hong Kong   Buenos Aires

It was the first chilly day in Care-a-lot.

An orange 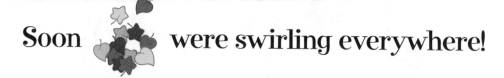 fell from the sky.

Then a bright red 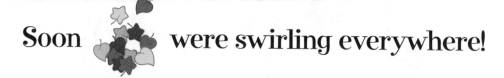 floated by.

Soon 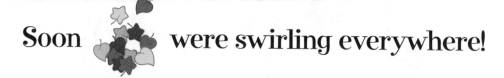 were swirling everywhere!

"Fall is here early!" 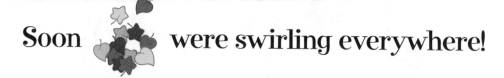 cheered.

"Let's have our Fall Festival!"

said  .

There was a lot to do to get ready.

 made a list in her .

"Do we have enough time?"

worried Grumpy Bear.

"If we all work together we will,"

 said.

Bedtime Bear went  picking

with  .

They loaded  into their

 .

"What fun!" said .

Bedtime Bear did not answer.

Good thing she brought her  !

Good Luck Bear drew faces.

He used a black  .

 baked a

huge  .

Tenderheart Bear tasted a  .

"Make sure you save some for the rest

of us!" laughed.

Good Luck Bear drew faces.

He used a black  .

 baked a

huge  .

Tenderheart Bear tasted a  .

"Make sure you save some for the rest

of us!"  laughed.

 were hanging

from the .

Harmony Bear climbed a  .

She sat on a  .

"Catch!" she shouted.

 caught an .

She put it in her  .

"Let's make  cider," said

Harmony Bear.

"It's the perfect fall drink," said

Friend Bear.

Harmony Bear squashed

the  .

Friend Bear caught the juice in

a  .

filled a with water.

She put in the extra .

"We can bob for ," she said.

She showed Love-a-lot Bear

how to play.

"I love this game!" Love-a-lot Bear said.

Tenderheart Bear and Grumpy Bear

made a  .

They stuffed his with .

They put his  on straight.

"Is he too scary?" worried Grumpy Bear.

"No, he's a cheery  !" Tenderheart

Bear said.

"Time for rides!" said

Champ Care Bear.

He filled up a  with .

He put on his  .

Then Champ Care Bear gave each

bear a turn.

"Time for the festival!"

 cheered.

The Fall Festival was perfect!

All the bears drank cider.

 gave  a

 of  .

Grumpy Bear played with

the cheery  .

And Love-a-lot Bear bobbed

for  .

"We did it!" said .

Just then a  landed on

Grumpy Bear's nose.

 smiled. "You know what that

means, don't you?"

"It's too early for a Winter Festival!"

Grumpy Bear said.

All the Care Bears laughed.

Did you spot all of the pictures in this picture clue reader? Each picture is on a flash card. Ask an adult to cut up the flash cards. Then try reading the words on the backs of the cards. The pictures will be your clues.

Reading is fun with the Care Bears!

Cheer Bear	leaf
notebook	Funshine Bear
pumpkin	Share Bear

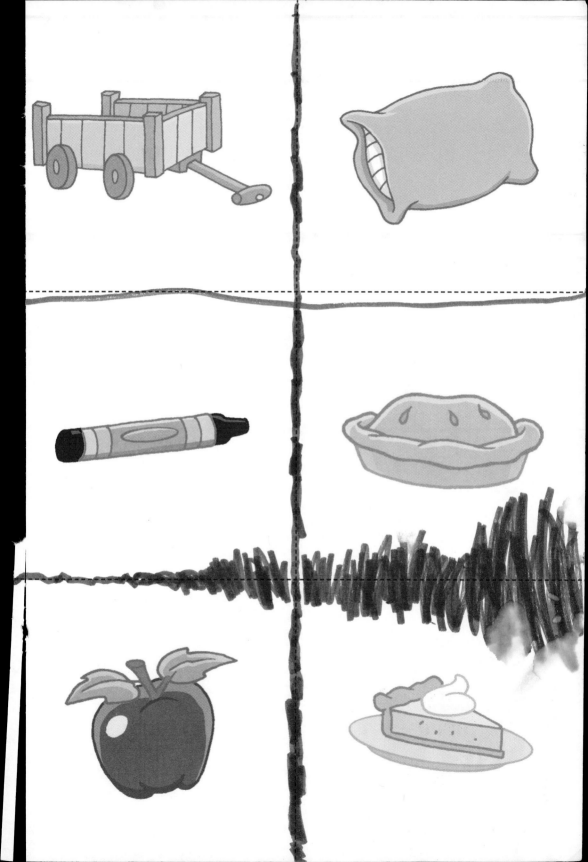

pillow	wagon
pie	crayon
slice	apple

ladder	tree
basket	branch
barrel	pitcher

shirt	scarecrow
hat	hay
snowflake	roller skates